CLEVER RACCOON

JANE THAYER • Illustrated by Holly Keller

Catherine Woolley ,pseud.

WILLIAM MORROW AND COMPANY • NEW YORK 1981

Text copyright © 1981 by Catherine Woolley
Illustrations copyright © 1981 by Holly Keller

Library of Congress Cataloging in Publication Data
Clever raccoon. Woolley, Catherine.
Summary: The people try to outwit the clever raccoon who is robbing their garden
of delicious fresh corn on the cob.
[1. Raccoons—Fiction] I. Keller, Holly. II. Title. PZ7.W882Cl   [E]   80-23119
ISBN 0-688-00238-2   ISBN 0-688-00239-0 (lib. bdg.)

For Sarah, with love.
J.T.
For Corey and Jesse.
H.K.

Squirrel and Chipmunk lived in a garden,
which they shared with some people,
and their friends Skunk and Raccoon
lived in the woods outside.
Squirrel didn't miss a thing that went on.
One day he said to Chipmunk,
"Those People are planting corn."

Chipmunk told Skunk, and Skunk told Raccoon.
Raccoon's eyes brightened,

because he loved corn
more than anything in the world.

He marked the date on his calendar
and told Mrs. Raccoon.

The people planted four rows of corn.
"We'll have fresh corn on the cob!" they said.
Their neighbor, next door,
was planning to plant corn too,
even though he knew raccoons love corn.
"Only one problem," he said. "Raccoons."
"We haven't seen a raccoon," the people protested.
"Wait," said the neighbor.

Squirrel preferred peanuts himself.

"Will Raccoon eat the corn?" Chipmunk asked nervously.

"*Will* you eat the corn?" Skunk inquired.

Raccoon looked mysterious.

Raccoon kept his calendar handy,
and at last one night he went and nibbled an ear of corn.
It wasn't quite ripe enough.

"Something has nibbled our corn!" the people exclaimed.

"Did you nibble?" said Skunk suspiciously to Raccoon.

Raccoon smiled.

"What do we do?" cried the people.

"Put up a fence," said their neighbor.

"I've planted my corn, and *I'm* going to put up a fence."

"Those People are putting up a fence,"
Squirrel told Chipmunk, who told Skunk, who told Raccoon.

Raccoon chuckled.

The corn grew, the kernels swelled, plump and milky,
and the people's mouths watered.
"Tomorrow the first row will be ripe!"
That night Raccoon consulted his calendar.
He climbed the people's fence and ate the whole row.

"The whole row is gone!" the people cried.

"How can we stop that raccoon?"

"Put a radio in the cornpatch at night.

That's what I'm going to do.

That will scare him away," said their neighbor.

"What's a radio?" Squirrel asked.

"Dangerous?" inquired Chipmunk.

"Radio?" asked Skunk cautiously.

Raccoon almost laughed out loud.

When the music was turned on, he danced a jig,

and soon Squirrel and Chipmunk were waltzing to the music

while Skunk tapped his toe.

That night Raccoon didn't go near the corn.

The next night he checked on another cornpatch.

"You were right," the people told their neighbor.

"Tomorrow we'll have

delicious fresh corn on the cob for dinner."

That night Raccoon and Mrs. Raccoon ate the whole row.

"You said the radio would keep him away!"
the people shouted.

"It did for a while," said their neighbor.

"Just until the corn was perfect!
We have two rows left.
What do we do?"

"Set a trap and bait it with peanut butter.
Raccoons like peanut butter," said their neighbor.

"It won't hurt the creature, and you can cart him away."

"What's a trap?" asked Squirrel.

"Dangerous?" asked Chipmunk nervously.

"A trap?" inquired Skunk.

Raccoon looked thoughtful.

Squirrel was going home at sunset

when he smelled peanuts.

Peanuts were to him what corn was to Raccoon.

He traced the smell to a kind of box with the door open.

In he pranced, and the moment he nibbled

down dropped the door, *clank*.

Squirrel was trapped.

When the people found

only a chattering squirrel in their trap,

they said, "Pardon us!"

Squirrel flounced off.

They reset the trap.

This time Chipmunk couldn't resist
that delicious smell, and he crept in.
Clank.
"We don't want you!" cried the people.
Chipmunk rushed out to tell his friends
about his horrible experience.
The third row of corn was almost ripe.
"We've got to catch that raccoon," said the people,

and they baited the trap
with a huge hunk of peanut butter.
But Squirrel and Chipmunk had learned their lesson.
And Raccoon was checking another cornpatch.
This time Skunk sniffed and stepped cautiously inside.
Clank.
When the people found a skunk in their trap,
they got away fast.

"What do we do?"
  Naturally, their neighbor knew.
"Speak softly, put a nice fat beetle outside,
  and raise the door gently."
  They found a fat, fresh beetle,
  spoke softly, and gently raised the door.
  Skunk had had a nap,
  he was hungry for his beetle breakfast,
  so he ate it and waddled off.
"Well," said the people, "we've caught everything else.
  Let's hope tonight will be raccoon night.
  At least, the third row of corn is almost ripe,
  and he hasn't touched it."
  They brought out an enormous peanut-butter sandwich.
"My first row is almost ripe, and he hasn't touched it,"
  said their neighbor with great satisfaction.
  Before he retired for the night,
  Squirrel passed a warning to Raccoon.

Next morning the people stared at their trap.

Squirrel stared too.

The trapdoor was down.

There was no squirrel in the trap.

No chipmunk in the trap.

No skunk in the trap.

No raccoon in the trap.

No peanut butter in the trap.

But that wasn't all.

The people rushed to the cornpatch.

Every ear of just-ripe corn in the third row

had been eaten up.

"He got the peanut butter and the corn too!"
 moaned the people.

"How did he get the peanut butter and escape?"
 For once their neighbor had no answer.

"When I went in and nibbled,
  the door clanked right down!" cried Squirrel.
"How did he get out?" demanded Chipmunk.
  The people decided to solve this mystery.
  They would bait the trap and hide.
  Squirrel was so mystified that he hid too
  and made Chipmunk come along.

They all waited, still as could be.
They waited and waited.
Maybe he wasn't coming.
There was a faint sound.
Here he comes.
In the moonlight they made out a bushy figure
approaching the trap.

Suddenly—a surprise. *A second raccoon*.
One was inside the trap.
The people flashed on their light,
and two surprised raccoons looked up.
Mrs. Raccoon was holding up the trapdoor
with her clever little raccoon hands.
Raccoon was coming out,
peanut butter in his mouth.

Mrs. Raccoon dropped the door.

Clank.

The Raccoons ambled off.

The people looked at each other.
Then, "Ha, ha, ha, ha, ha! Ho, ho, ho, ho, ho!
Whoever thought of *two* raccoons?
They're smarter than we are, wiser than that wise guy.
Come on, let's pick our last row of corn
before it's just right for raccoons!"

Then Squirrel chattered at Chipmunk,
"Why didn't you hold the door?"
Chipmunk chirped, "Why didn't you?"

Mrs. Raccoon complained, "I was looking forward to corn."

Raccoon paused in the moonlight to consult his calendar.

"Cheer up, dear," he said.

"That wise guy's row will be ripe tomorrow night!"